S0-AAA-255

Bantam Skylark Books in the Time Traveler series
Ask your bookseller for the book you have missed

Time Traveler 1: VOYAGE WITH COLUMBUS
by Seymour Reit
illustrated by José Gonzales Navaroo

Time Traveler 2: THE LEGEND OF HIAWATHA
by Carol Gaskin
illustrated by José Ortiz

2

Time Traveler™

The Legend of Hiawatha

by Carol Gaskin
illustrated by José Ortiz

A Byron Preiss Book

A BANTAM SKYLARK BOOK®
TORONTO • NEW YORK • LONDON • SYDNEY • AUCKLAND

RL 3, 007-010

THE LEGEND OF HIAWATHA
A Bantam Skylark Book / November 1986

Special thanks to Judy Gitenstein,
Anne Greenberg, Robin Stevenson, and
Bruce Stevenson.

Book design by Alex Jay
Cover painting by John Palencar
Cover design by Alex Jay
Mechanicals by Mary LeCleir
Typesetting by David E. Seham Associates, Inc.

Editor: Ruth Ashby

ISBN 0-553-15450-8

Published simultaneously in the United States and Canada

Bantam Books are published by Bantam Books, Inc. Its trade-mark, consisting of the words "Bantam Books" and the portrayal of a rooster, is Registered in U.S. Patent and Trademark Office and in other countries. Marca Registrada. Bantam Books, Inc., 666 Fifth Avenue, New York, New York 10103.

PRINTED IN THE UNITED STATES OF AMERICA

S 0 9 8 7 6 5 4 3 2 1

Welcome, Time Traveler!

This book is your time machine. It is not like any book you've ever read. When you turn the page, you will travel back to one of the most exciting times in American history. You will meet Hiawatha, a great leader of the Iroquois Indians.

In every Time Traveler book you will be given a mission to complete while you are back in time. In this book you will be there at the founding of the Iroquois League of Five Nations.

Every few pages you will get to make a choice about what to do next. If you want help along the way, you can read the information about Hiawatha and the Iroquois in the next few pages.

Now you're ready for your adventure. Turn the page and find out your mission.

Your Mission

Your mission is to meet the Indian leader Hiawatha and be part of the founding of the Iroquois League of Five Nations. As proof that you've completed your mission, you must bring back a bead of Hiawatha's wampum belt.

In the middle of the sixteenth century, five separate tribes made up the group called the Iroquois nation. These tribes, whose territory covered most of eastern North America, frequently fought among themselves.

One of their great chieftans, Hiawatha, wanted to bring an end to the wars that divided his people. With his help the tribes banded together at a great council meeting and formed the League of Five Nations.

As part of your mission you must find Hiawatha and win his trust. To do so, you will learn all about Iroquois ways—by becoming an Iroquois yourself!

To start the Time Machine, turn the page.

You are traveling back in time.

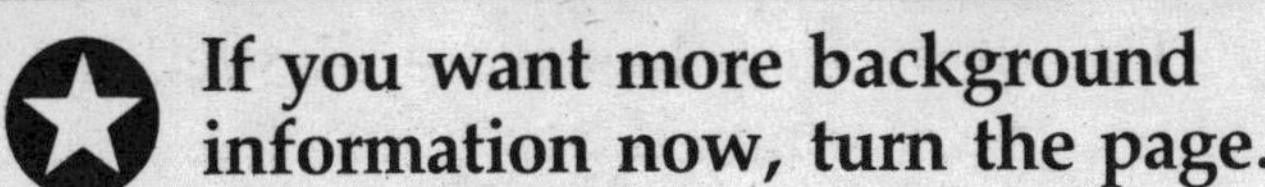

★ If you want more background information now, turn the page.

★ If you are ready to start your mission now, turn to page 1.

The World of Hiawatha

Before you begin your mission, here is some information you'll need about Hiawatha and the Iroquois.

Five tribes make up the group of people known as the Iroquois: the Senecas, the Cayugas, the Onondagas, the Oneidas, and the Mohawks. The name Iroquois is a French word. The tribes called themselves the People of the Longhouse, after their long narrow dwellings.

The Iroquois had their villages in what is today New York State. Their trails were clearly marked and used regularly by hunting and war parties. The routes were so well chosen that they eventually became the basis for the New York State Thruway. Their territory, where they hunted and traveled, stretched from Canada to the Tennessee River, and from New England to the Mississippi.

The Iroquois tribes were divided into clans, which were named for animals—Deer, Wolf, Bear, Beaver, Turtle, and so on. Clans were like large families. If you were a member of the Deer clan, for example, you were related as if by blood to all the other members of the Deer clan.

Tobacco was considered sacred and played an important role in the Iroquois religious and healing ceremonies. In their personal code of conduct bravery was respected above all else.

For many years the five tribes fought each other—brothers against brothers. Many people were killed. During this awful period starvation was widespread because hunters feared going outside their tribal hunting boundaries.

Amidst this strife and bloodshed a great leader emerged—Hiawatha!

According to Iroquois legend, Hiawatha was living alone in the forest when Deganawida, a seer of the future and a reader of dreams, had a vision of peace. Hiawatha was so inspired by this vision that he became Deganawida's disciple. Hiawatha was even able to convince the terrible war-chief Atotarho to join the way of peace, and eventually all the tribes came together in a great council meeting to establish the League of Five Nations.

The strength and success of the Iroquois League was much admired by the American colonists, and some historians even think it may have been the model for the American Constitution and the democratic system.

We don't know just when Hiawatha lived nor do we know the exact date the Iroquois League

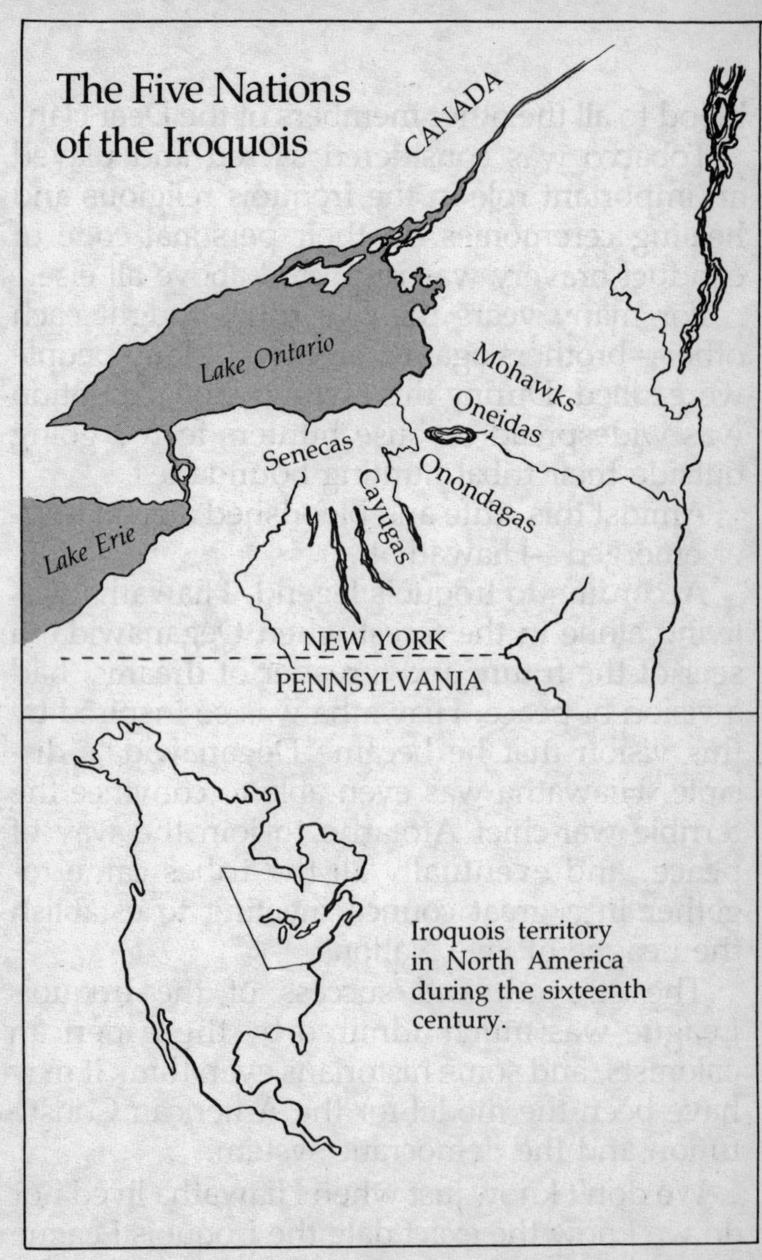

Iroquois territory in North America during the sixteenth century.

of Five Nations was founded. It began sometime between 1400 and 1600. In this book we've used 1550 as an approximate date.

Some people say that Hiawatha was a member of the Onondaga tribe. Others say he was born a Mohawk and later was adopted by the Onondagas. While the facts of his life will forever remain a mystery, we know that Hiawatha was a great leader, indeed. The bond of peace that he helped forge in the League of Five Nations lasted for centuries.

The Hiawatha in the book you are reading was an important figure in Iroquois legend. He is *not* the Indian of Henry Wadsworth Longfellow's famous 1855 poem, *Song of Hiawatha*. That Hiawatha was a member of the Ojibway tribe of the northern Great Lakes.

The Iroquois valued beads of wampum, or shell, which they strung or wove into belts to record important agreements. Like other useful objects, wampum was accepted in trade for land or furs. It was with wampum beads that Hiawatha wove a belt on which he recorded the treaty of the League of Five Nations so that his people would never forget the promises they had made. That belt still exists today.

Now you are ready to start your mission. Turn the page.

1

The year is 1530. You are standing in an Onondaga village at dawn. In the woodlands surrounding the village, birds chirp merrily to greet the new day. You walk toward the nearest building. It is a long wooden house with a curved roof, covered all over with crusty brown tree bark.

There are a dozen more of these longhouses built on either side of a path that runs through the middle of the village. Inside the longhouses people are just beginning to stir.

Suddenly the birds stop singing. Freezing in your steps, you listen to the silence. You hear a strange whistling sound from the woods beyond the village. *ZZZZZingg!* A blazing arrow streaks over your head, flying toward the longhouse roof. *Tha-wump!* The arrow finds its mark, and the papery bark bursts into flames! *Thwump! Thwump!* Two more houses catch fire!

Shouting and coughing, the Onondagas run from their burning longhouses. "It's a raid!" they cry.

Zing! Zing! The hidden attackers shower the frightened Onondagas with arrows. A woman yanks an arrow from a wall and studies its feathers. "Mohawks!" she yells. "Run!"

The Onondaga women flee with their children as the men ready their bows and war clubs for battle. You spin toward the woods, hoping to catch sight of a Mohawk.

One glance is enough. A band of Mohawk warriors is headed your way! They are wearing a sort of armor made of sticks or reeds. Their faces are painted with stripes and their tomahawks are raised and ready. *ZZing!* A Mohawk arrow barely misses your cheek! You'd better take cover!

Hurry! Turn to page 6.

3

It is the winter of 1550. You are walking through a pine forest, hoping to find an Iroquois village.

It's cold! The forest floor is covered with a foot of snow, and your feet break through the icy crust as you walk.

It is hard to tell if you are following a path. Everything is black and white—the birch trees, the snowy pines—except for the icicles, which glisten a silvery gray.

As the trail widens, you spot fresh footprints in the snow. Perhaps they belong to an Iroquois!

You follow them into a grove of pines. Suddenly you trip and fall headlong into the snow. Brushing yourself off, you keep going.

A short time later you find yourself in a grove of pines again. There is a hole in the snow. It is the hole you made when you fell. You have been following your own footprints!

Behind you, a voice laughs merrily. You turn to see a tall Indian boy dressed in deerskin and furs. He carries a bow and a quiver filled with arrows. He is wearing snowshoes and he does not sink into the snow at all.

"Are you tracking a bear?" he asks, still laughing. "Or are you lost?"

"I am looking for an Onondaga village," you reply. Then you laugh, too. "But I guess I've been tracking myself!"

"I am an Onondaga," the boy says. "My name is Redwing. You are brave to travel in this forest by yourself. My tribe welcomes young braves. But what do you seek in my village?"

"I am looking for a man called Hiawatha," you tell Redwing. "Do you know him?"

Redwing looks at you curiously. "Yes," he says. "But Hiawatha has left my people to live in the wilderness. He is a hermit, and he speaks to no one."

"Where can I find him?" you ask.

"It is said he lives in this very forest," answers Redwing, "somewhere in the hills. But it is a dangerous journey. And you have no snowshoes. Or a bow! Why not return to my village with me? My people can help you."

Do you want to continue your search for Hiawatha on your own? Turn to page 12.

Do you want to go with Redwing? Turn to page 19.

The Mohawk raiders reach the village as a building falls in a roar of flames and smoke. You spot a boy about your own age as he dives behind a huge pile of pumpkins heaped next to one of the longhouses.

Running for your life, you leap behind the pile of pumpkins. You come face-to-face with the Onondaga boy—and the arrow he has aimed at your throat!

"Wait!" you cry. "I am not a Mohawk! I mean you no harm!"

The boy keeps his bow taut, but he does not shoot. You are not sure he believes you, but right now you do not care. For there is a *real* Mohawk creeping up behind him from the side of the longhouse. And the Mohawk is holding a wooden war club with a mean-looking spike in its end.

"Look out!" you yell, knocking the boy into the heap of pumpkins. You grab one of the pumpkins and heave it at your attacker.

The pumpkin hits the warrior square in the chest and sends him flying against the wall of the longhouse. His tomahawk falls with a thud as he slumps to the ground.

7

The Onondaga boy scrambles to his feet. "He would have taken me prisoner! I have much to thank you for."

The boy takes a leather strap from the unconscious Mohawk brave and uses it to tie the warrior's wrists together.

Peering over the heap of pumpkins, you see several Onondagas, captured by Mohawks and tied the same way. They are being led away into the forest by the Mohawk raiders.

"Now we will have a prisoner of our own!" the boy says proudly. "If this Mohawk is a brave man, he will be adopted as an Onondaga, to live with a clan that has lost a son. Perhaps he will join the Turtle clan—that is my family—for we lost a brave warrior only last month."

He eyes you with curiosity.

"What clan are you?" he asks. "You don't look like you're from our tribe. But you are *certainly* brave enough to be adopted! How are you called? My name is Hiawatha."

Hiawatha! Could you have found him so easily? But this boy is just a year or two older than you. If he's the right Hiawatha, you're about twenty years too early.

"I am a traveler from a distant place," you say. "I am searching for a great treasure called wampum. Have you ever heard of it?"

"I have never heard of it, friend," Hiawatha answers. "But you will make a fine Onondaga if you choose to stay here."

Oh well, you think. Hiawatha would not have heard of wampum if he hadn't created it yet. But you don't want to stay in 1530. Hiawatha is too young—and the wars are too dangerous!

You could jump far ahead of the wars and try to learn more of Hiawatha's story. Someone might be able to tell you just where Hiawatha was when he discovered wampum. Or you could jump forward twenty years to search the Iroquois villages for an older Hiawatha.

"I am honored to have met you," you tell Hiawatha, "but I must be on my way."

"Good luck, then," Hiawatha replies. "Who knows? Perhaps we will meet again."

Waving good-bye to Hiawatha, you slip into the woods and jump forward in time.

Do you want to jump ahead twenty years to find Hiawatha again? Turn to page 3.

Do you want to jump ahead 250 years to try to learn more of his story? Turn to page 13.

10

It is 1650. You are walking along a forest trail where Redwing's village used to be.

Ahead of you, a man is trudging through the woods. He wears woolen clothes and a fur hat. Over one shoulder he carries a huge sack. It is bulging with animal skins.

"Hello!" you call. The man turns and smiles. His beard is so bushy it could easily clothe a whole raccoon.

"Hello!" he answers, dropping the heavy sack. Then he, too, drops to the ground. "Will you rest with me awhile? I am Hendrick, from Amsterdam—and now from *New* Amsterdam."

"You must be a fur trapper," you say, pointing to the sack.

"Oh, no," answers Hendrick. "The Indians trap them. Then I trade for them. And a fine trade it is, too! The English and my fellow Dutchmen can't get enough beaver hats—they're very popular, you know. Where are *you* headed?"

"I am looking for an Iroquois village," you answer.

"Ah, then you are a trader as well?" asks

Hendrick. "I trade often with the great League of Five Nations."

"Actually, I have nothing to trade," you say. "I am hoping to . . ."

"But of course! I understand," Hendrick says with a wink. "You are just getting started in the fur trade. You will need some of these wampum beads." He pulls a handful of purple and white beads from a pouch at his belt.

"The Iroquois love these beads as much as white men love furs." He laughs. "But if you have no wampum, I will give you a piece of advice. The Iroquois respect courage above all else. If you want them to respect you, you must show them that you are very brave."

If wampum is being used for trade already, then you are much too late to meet Hiawatha. You remember what Redwing told you about bravery. Perhaps you made a mistake to run away. You decide to return to Redwing's village and run the gauntlet.

"Thank you for your help," you tell Hendrick. You set off once again.

Jump back 100 years and run the gauntlet. Turn to page 16.

You decide to set off on your own to search for Hiawatha. You start off in the direction of the hills beyond the pine grove. The ground is slippery, and soon you are shivering. Once, you glimpse a deer through the trees, but you make so much noise crunching through the snow that the deer swiftly disappears.

You trip again, turning your ankle on a twisted root that was buried in the snow.

You wish you could light a fire, but you have no matches. Maybe you should have gone with Redwing. You trudge on.

"Had enough?" says a voice behind you.

It is Redwing. You are glad to see him!

"You are quite an adventurer!" Redwing says. "But it is a long way to the home of Hiawatha. You do not know the ways of the forest, and when night falls, the spirits of the wood lurk about. Why not come with me?"

"Thank you," you say gratefully.

"First, we will have to find you some snowshoes." Redwing laughs. "You crash through the snow like a bear!"

Follow Redwing to the Onondaga village. Turn to page 19.

It's December 16, 1773. You are standing in front of a row of shops in a narrow, unpaved street. Men trot by on horseback, wearing long coats over tight trousers. Their long hair is tied into ponytails beneath three-cornered hats.

You must be in a colonial town!

You see a yellowish light coming from a shop across the street. You can just make out the sign in the window:

EDES & GILL

Printers

Peering through the shop window, you let out a gasp. The shop is full of Indians!

Suddenly a young man taps you on the shoulder. "Hurry inside if you want to join the Mohawks," he whispers. "It's almost dark!"

Mohawks? What are they doing here? You follow the colonist into the shop to find out.

None of the Indians pay much attention to you. Most of them are wearing blankets and several are painting their faces with war paint. *War paint?*

"Why are they painting their faces?" you ask the young colonist.

"How else should we dress to raid Boston Harbor?" He laughs and unwraps the bundle he is carrying. It's a hatchet!

Before you can ask him what is going on, a cry goes up in the room.

"No taxation without representation! To Griffin's wharf! To the sea with England's tea!"

The Indians holler and whoop and begin to stream out the door of the shop. You walk with them to Griffin's wharf, where you board a great wooden ship called the *Dartmouth*.

The Indians' shoes clatter on the ship's deck as they drag crate after wooden crate from the hold. Then you notice that most of the Mohawks are wearing leather shoes with big square buckles.

These are not Indians! They are colonists *dressed* as Indians. They are using their "tomahawks" to chop open the wooden crates, which are overflowing with flaky brown tea. The colonists throw the crates of tea overboard.

There are no real Indians here. You have come too far in time. You are witnessing the *Boston Tea Party*!

Jump back to 1550. Turn to page 3.

You are about to run the gauntlet. Taking a deep breath, you charge between the two lines of Onondaga women.

Swish! Swat! They lash at you lightly with the sapling whips. But you do not cry out, and soon you reach the end of the lines.

Redwing lets out a whoop of glee as tribe members gather around you. Their welcome is so friendly that you feel wonderful.

"I knew you would be brave!" says Redwing. "You have passed your first test. Now you will live with the Onondagas and learn our ways. If you do well, you will be adopted into our tribe and given a new name. But until then, you will live in the longhouse of the Turtle clan. Come, meet my family."

Redwing leads you into a longhouse. The bark door swings open at the top. Inside, it is dark. As your eyes grow used to the dim light, you can see at once how the longhouse got its name—it is longer than a bowling alley! Everything is made of wood or bark, hide or fur. It is like being inside a giant tree turned on its side.

Both sides of the house are lined with sleeping alcoves. In each alcove, a platform has been built a few feet off the earthen floor. The platforms are strewn with furs and look warm and cozy.

"Each family shares one alcove," Redwing explains.

Every fifteen feet or so, the alcoves are separated from their neighbors by a bark-walled storage compartment. Above the alcoves are shelves. You can see baskets and bowls, bows and arrows, snowshoes and paddles, all neatly stored away. Dried apples and braids of corn hang from the rafters.

Between each set of alcoves is a cooking fire. The smoke rises through holes in the roof. You stop near a fire. Something tasty is bubbling in a pot.

"Two or four families share a hearth," Redwing goes on.

"And I am sure you are hungry!" says a young girl. She is as tall as Redwing and appears to be a year or two older.

"This is my sister, Rainbow," says Redwing.

"We eat only one meal together, at midmorning," Rainbow tells you. "The rest of the time, you must help yourself when you are hungry." She hands you a bowl of the good-smelling food. It is corn soup, and it tastes as sweet as yellow corn in the middle of summer.

"Tomorrow we shall go fishing," says Rainbow as you eat, "and I'll teach you to paddle a canoe. We will bring back a fish for the great New Year's festival."

"If you come hunting with me," says Redwing, "I'll show you how to shoot an arrow as straight as a pine, and we'll bring back a bear for the New Year's festival!"

The longhouse grows crowded and noisy as the Turtle clan gets ready for sleep. Soon you are snuggled down beneath a thick bearskin and listening to the yawns and snores from the other alcoves.

You wake up at dawn. Redwing and Rainbow are waiting for you.

Do you want to go hunting with Redwing? Turn to page 22.

Do you want to go fishing with Rainbow? Turn to page 29.

You set off with Redwing for his village. Soon you reach the edge of the forest, and the Onondaga boy whistles sharply.

"Now my people will expect us," he explains. "They will know I am bringing a captive."

"A captive?" you say. "B-but . . ."

"Don't worry." Redwing smiles. "I know they will want to adopt you when they see your courage."

You're not sure you like the sound of this, but you follow Redwing through a cornfield and up a hill to his village. It is hidden by a towering fence made of huge, sharpened logs.

"The palisades are for protection," explains Redwing. "There is an opening over here." He leads you into the village.

You have only a moment to admire the rows of longhouses in Redwing's village before you are surrounded by a crowd of Onondagas. They smile at you kindly and seem happy to meet you.

"Redwing's prisoner looks very brave," says a woman, poking your arm.

"You must be tired after your long journey," says another, pinching your cheek.

"Are you hungry, young one?" asks a third, pulling your hair.

"Hey, ouch!" you say. "What's going on?"

The village women form two lines, facing one another. They are holding sapling switches that they crack like whips.

"It is our custom that newcomers run the gauntlet," Redwing tells you. "Don't worry, you'll be fine."

You are not sure that you'll be fine. Do you trust Redwing? What if they mean to hurt you? You can still run for cover and jump forward in time. But then you might not meet Hiawatha.

Do you jump ahead 100 years? Turn to page 10.

Do you run the gauntlet? Turn to page 16.

You decide to go hunting with Redwing. It is a chilly winter dawn. As you and Redwing climb into the hills, the snow grows deeper.

"Put these on," says Redwing. He hands you a pair of snowshoes. They are about three feet long and are made of bentwood and leather. Redwing shows you how they fasten onto your moccasins with leather straps. You feel as if you have tennis racquets strapped to your feet! At first you have trouble walking, but before you know it, you are skimming along the surface of the snow.

"Let's stop for an archery lesson," Redwing says, grinning. He bends his bow and lets an arrow fly. It sails into the air and lodges in a tree with a *thwomp!*

Now it's your turn. You set an arrow onto the bowstring and try to pull the string back to your chin. It's hard to bend the bow! Losing your grip, you let the arrow go—right into the ground, a few feet from your toes.

Redwing laughs. "Not bad for a first try!" he

says. "It takes even our strongest braves years of practice to be able to shoot straight. Let's go!"

You walk for two hours. Finally, Redwing stops in a clearing.

"We'll build a fire and rest," he says, as you begin to gather pieces of wood. You sit at the crackling fire, hoping your frozen fingers will soon thaw.

Then Redwing hops to his feet. "Now we will build our bear trap. We must dig a deep pit in the snow."

"But the earth will be frozen and too hard to dig," you say.

Redwing laughs and points to a huge fallen tree. There is a deep pit in the earth where the roots have torn free.

"We'll fill the hole with loose snow," Redwing says, "so it looks level with the ground. When an animal falls into the pit, we'll snare him in this net." He shows you a folded net that he carries on his back.

You and Redwing work hard to fill the deep pit with snow. Then you settle down by the fire to wait.

"I'm going to look for more firewood," Redwing tells you. "Keep watch until I return."

You nod, staring into the fire. After a while, your eyelids begin to droop.

Suddenly you hear a low growl. Your eyes blink open. *It's a bear!*

A gigantic brown bear is lumbering into the clearing, several yards from Redwing's trap. He sniffs the air and stops when he sees the fire. Is he afraid of the flames?

You reach for a log that is flaming at one end like a torch. The bear takes a step in your direction.

Do you want to use the burning log to try to frighten the bear into the trap? Turn to page 28.

Do you want to back out of the clearing and into the forest? Turn to page 26.

Dropping the torch, you quickly back out of the clearing and into the forest. Then you turn and run.

You hear a thundering howl. It's the bear! Is he caught in the trap? Or is he after you? You keep running!

The forest is dark and cold. The pines cast long shadows on the silent snow. An owl screeches overhead. In no time, you are lost.

You decide to look for the trail to the clearing. There is an opening in the trees ahead of you. You enter a small grove.

In the spooky light, a twisted, whitish face leers at you from the center of a tree trunk! Its eyes are round and crazy, its nose is pulled to one side of its face, and its rubbery mouth is laughing and frowning at the same time. A masked spirit of the forest!

Spinning around to run away, your snowshoe catches on a tree root and you slam into the rough trunk of an oak.

Then you remember nothing.

Turn to page 33.

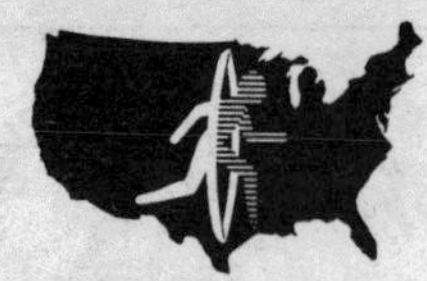

You grab the burning torch from the fire and wave it at the bear.

The bear backs away from the flame, toward the snowy pit.

"One more step, now." *It's Redwing!* He is standing behind the pit, holding his net.

You push the fiery torch toward the bear. Growling fiercely, the bear turns toward Redwing, then lurches forward, and plummets headlong into the pit!

Redwing throws his net over the bear. The clearing fills with whooping Onondagas.

"I met with another hunting party!" Redwing calls to you. The huntsmen make short work of the struggling bear. Then they haul him from the pit and load him onto a wooden sled.

"We will surely have the best New Year's festival ever!" cries Redwing. "And it will be thanks to you—a great hunter!"

You help pull the heavy sled back to the village. The people greet you joyfully, and the whole village joins in the plans for the feast.

Turn to page 41.

You decide to go fishing with Rainbow. She hands you a large net, neatly folded into a tight bundle. "Here is the fishing net," she says excitedly. "And here is your paddle."

You follow Rainbow to a bubbling stream. A bark canoe lies on the bank. You are surprised at how light it is as you help Rainbow put it into the water.

You climb into the canoe and sit down at the back while Rainbow stands in the stern to paddle. In time with her strokes, you dip your paddle first to one side and then to the other. The canoe zips silently through the water.

You pass a row of trees with narrow chutes driven into their bases. There is something dripping slowly from the chutes into little bark tubs that look like miniature canoes.

"Those are sugar maple trees," Rainbow explains, following your gaze. "The sap will be boiled down to make maple sugar."

Soon you notice chunks of ice floating in the stream.

"With this early thaw, the fish should be running as well as the sap," says Rainbow. "We'll catch a trout for the New Year's festival!"

A sheet of ice spans the stream ahead of you, so you leave the canoe on shore and continue on foot. Rainbow carries the net and a pole and you carry a basket to hold the fish.

You come to a spot where thick ice lines both sides of the stream. But a channel of running water has carved a path through the middle of the ice.

"We'll try here," says Rainbow, carefully walking out onto the ice. She stares intently into the running water. You see a glint of silver in the morning sun.

"There's one!" Rainbow cries. She casts her line into the icy stream, then jerks it swiftly from the water. She nets the thrashing fish with her other hand. You see flashes of icy blue, silver, yellow, and red, as droplets of water spill through the net, dripping from the fins and tail of the fish.

"You caught a beauty!" you shout.

"It's a brook trout," says Rainbow. "A good-sized one, too."

The trout is the most beautiful fish you have ever seen. Its blue-green back merges to silver on its sides, and it is speckled all over with yellow and red spots. Rainbow turns the fish into your basket and frees her net.

"Now it's your turn!" she says. "Cast the net quickly if you see a flash of silver. And don't get too near the edge of the ice."

Rainbow steps back onto the bank of the stream to watch. You can hear the brook trout flapping against the sides of the basket.

Standing as close to the edge of the ice as you dare, you stare into the stream for a long time. Once, you catch a glimpse of silver and cast the net into the water. But you pull it up empty and wonder if the sunlight is playing tricks with your eyes.

Suddenly you see it again. A flash of silvery blue. It's a trout! It must be two feet long—even larger than Rainbow's!

You concentrate on the fish. Rainbow's voice breaks into your thoughts.

"Quickly! The basket—*it's floating away!*"

The basket has slipped through the ice and is floating rapidly downstream. Upstream, the trout is swimming your way.

Do you want to try to net the basket?
Turn to page 35.

Do you want to try to net the fish?
Turn to page 39.

You wake up freezing and feverish, and you're not sure where you are. You are lying beneath something heavy. You stroke warm fur and realize it's a bearskin.

Raising yourself up onto one elbow, you squint into the dim light of a little room. Everything is made of wood, hide, and bark. There is a door in one wall. A low fire is burning in the center of an earthen floor.

You remember the Onondagas. You remember blacking out. But what is this room? It's not a longhouse.

Suddenly the door bangs open. Strange beings enter. Their faces are stretched and twisted, and their hair springs wildly from their heads. They wag their heads back and forth, ogling you with great, round eyes.

Are you dreaming? Is this a nightmare? You begin to shiver with fear.

One of the beings shakes a rattle over you from head to toe. The rattle is made of a turtle's shell. The being hums in a low, quaking voice. Then he begins to chant.

The others echo his eerie song as they dance around the fire. They moan and wail. One of the beings takes a pouch from his belt and crumbles some dried leaves onto the fire. You smell burning tobacco.

The figure with the rattle leans over you. His face is horrible. His eyes are huge and drooping. His nose is pushed over to one side of his face. And his mouth is puckered into a crooked *O,* as though he is about to whistle. He blows hot ashes onto your face and chest. You pull away and draw the bearskin up to your chin.

He snatches the cover from your shivering body and grabs you by the wrist!

The other beings beckon weirdly. They want you to join their dance around the fire.

Do you run for the door? Turn to page 40.

Do you join their dance? Turn to page 36.

Casting your net downstream, you snag the floating basket and pull it to safety.

"Hurrah!" shouts Rainbow. "You have saved our New Year's feast!"

"But I lost the biggest trout I have ever seen," you wail.

"Don't worry," Rainbow tells you. "What good would our fishing trip be if we didn't return with a story? Besides, everything looks bigger under water."

Laughing, you return to the canoe. Rainbow loads the prized brook trout into the little craft, and you set off for the village.

"We caught this fish together," says Rainbow. "If you hadn't acted so quickly, we would be returning empty-handed. This will be the best New Year ever!"

Turn to page 41.

You begin to dance around the fire.

"Who are you?" you whisper to the strange beings as they dance and moan.

"We are the False Face Company," says the being with the rattle. "Dance with us and you shall be healed."

You dance and dance. The fire smokes and flickers.

You feel dizzy; once, you almost fall. You are allowed to rest, and then you dance some more. Finally your fever breaks, and your head clears.

You notice that the False Faces wear leggings and moccasins and their horrible faces are wooden masks, painted or polished to a fine sheen. They are Onondaga medicine men!

"The False Face spirits cause illness," the one with the turtle rattle tells you. "So we wear their faces to cure these ills. Now you have been cured by the False Face Company. You will become one of us."

The Faces file out the door. You see that you are in a small hut. The doorkeeper is the last to leave.

"Sleep now, brave one," she says, lifting her mask. It is an old woman who smiles kindly at you as she passes through the door. "You must be strong to help us celebrate the New Year," she whispers.

You drift into a deep sleep, filled with dreams of bears and fish, canoes and arrows.

You awaken feeling strong and well, and as excited as if it were your birthday.

Turn to page 41.

Letting Rainbow's basket float away, you lean out over the ice to cast your net at the shining fish.

"I'll get the basket!" shouts Rainbow.

Crraaack! The ice crumbles beneath your feet! You fall into the icy stream. Your net pulls as your head starts to swim.

Then you remember nothing.

Turn to page 33.

You jump to your feet and head for the door. One of the beings blocks your way!

"You cannot pass by the doorkeeper," he says in a croaking voice.

The doorkeeper's hair is scraggly and white. A thick red tongue hangs almost to his chin, surrounded by sharp little teeth. His eyes are wild.

You decide to take his word for it and join the dance.

Turn to page 36.

The day of the New Year's festival has arrived. The entire village buzzes with excitement.

Redwing and Rainbow pull you from your warm bed in the Turtle longhouse.

"We'll have bear to eat and fresh trout and more!" they cry. "Get up, sleepyhead!"

Excited, you tumble out of bed and join the others by the fire.

"Soon you shall come to the dream-guessing ceremony," says Rainbow. "If you have a dream, you must tell it, or bad luck may befall us. Now we give thanks to the Maker of Life."

You and the other members of the Turtle clan sing a song of thanksgiving.

"Before the dream-guessing, we'll go begging!" say Redwing and Rainbow. They hand you a mask made of woven corn husks that form a fringe of wild hair, like a lion's mane. You are joined by several others, all masked.

You run from house to house, begging for treats. It's just like Halloween!

All over the village the Onondagas are singing. You watch a group of warriors perform the Great Feather dance. They wear their finest costumes, with feathered headdresses and necklaces of bears' claws. Their clothes are embroidered with porcupine quills.

Next, Redwing and Rainbow bring you to the center of the village.The Onondagas are gathered in a circle.

"This is an important occasion," they tell you. "It is a naming and adoption ceremony."

It's for you! As the Onondaga villagers chant and sing, an old woman beckons you. You recognize her from Redwing's longhouse. She is the head of the Turtle clan.

"From this day forward, you will belong to the Turtle clan," she says. "We are your mothers and fathers, your brothers and sisters. Your new name shall be New Eyes, for everything you see is for the first time. Thanks be to the Maker of Life."

Then she lowers something about your neck. It is a small wooden turtle, carved of dark wood and hung on a leather thong. Your heart swells with pride. You are an Iroquois!

The singing and dancing begin again. But your thoughts turn to your real purpose for being there. You have completed part of your mission. You have become an Iroquois. But have you learned enough of Iroquois ways to continue your search for Hiawatha?

"Soon it will be time for the dream-guessing," says Rainbow. "We tell our dreams with hints and clues. Someone else must guess the dream, or bad luck will come. Will you help, New Eyes?"

You know the dream-guessing ceremony is important. You are about to go when Redwing calls you. He is carrying a ball made of deerskin and two long nets fastened to wooden handles. They look like loose snowshoes.

"Come play lacrosse," he says. "The Turtle clan needs help against the Bears."

Do you want to help at the dream-guessing ceremony? Turn to page 46.

Do you want to play a game of lacrosse? Turn to page 49.

"Thank you, but I don't smoke," you say.

His eyes narrow and he looks at you with suspicion. Slowly, he reaches for his bow and arrows with one hand, while he throws a pinch of tobacco onto the fire with the other.

"For the spirits of the forest," he murmurs. The tobacco crackles and sends a puff of smoke into the air.

Deganawida fixes an arrow in his bow and points it at you.

"Are you a spirit of the forest?" he demands. "For no member of our tribe would refuse the sacred tobacco leaves. If you do not need to make peace with the spirits of the forest, perhaps you are one of them."

"N-no," you say, backing away.

"Or perhaps you are a *witch!*" shouts Deganawida. "Begone, witch!"

You run into the forest. There's no time to look—you leap far into the future!

Turn to page 58.

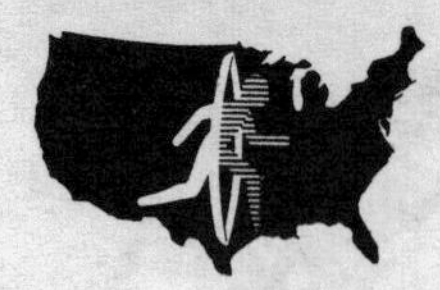

You enter a smoky longhouse for the dream-guessing ceremony.

The Onondagas are seated around a fire. Someone throws a pinch of tobacco on the fire and hums a sacred song.

"I have a dream to tell," says Rainbow. The room falls silent. "Here is my dream," she says. "It whistles from a tree."

"You dreamed of a bird," guesses a woman.

"An owl?" suggests a young man.

"I know," says an old man. "You dreamed of a False Face mask. A whistling mask, carved by an Onondaga on the trunk of a tree."

"You have guessed my dream," says Rainbow.

An ancient woman rises and begins to speak.

"What crawls on the earth is tangled in the sky," she says. "And my eyes see only red."

The room is very quiet. Then the Onondagas begin to guess.

"Red is the color of war," says one.

"Snakes crawl on the earth," says another.

"I can guess your dream," says a young

woman. "You dreamed of the wizard Atotarho, whose hair is a tangle of snakes. They say his mind is as tangled as his hair. He wants us to make war again. There are war parties in the forest. And the people are afraid."

"You have guessed my dream, young one," says the old woman. A shiver of fear passes through the room as she sits down.

"Here is my dream," says a Beaver brave. "I am full of holes, yet I will not sink."

"I can guess your dream!" you say. "You dreamed of a snowshoe. It is full of holes, but it keeps you from sinking in the snow!"

"You have guessed my dream, New Eyes." The brave smiles as he sits down.

The room is quiet. "Is that all?" asks the old man.

"I have one more dream," says the elderly woman. She rises once again. "I live in the forest. I have many teeth."

"A bear?" guesses Rainbow.

"A wolf?" says a brave of the Wolf clan.

The room is silent for a long time. Then Redwing leaps to his feet.

"I can guess your dream," he says. "You have dreamed of our brother, Hiawatha, whose name means He Who Combs. For does not a comb have many teeth? And does he not live in the forest?"

"You have guessed my dream, clever Redwing," says the old woman. "Now let us feast!"

You join the villagers in a feast such as you have never seen. You taste bear and trout, venison and corn cakes.

But as the Onondagas rejoice in the New Year, you turn to your Turtle brother and sister.

"You have taught me much about your ways," you tell them. "I am ready to continue my search for Hiawatha."

"Few have seen Hiawatha since he left our village," says Redwing. "I cannot tell you where to find him."

"Then I must look for him myself."

"You must be very careful, New Eyes," Rainbow says sadly. "For the tribes are at war, and the forest is dangerous."

"I wish you luck, friend," says Redwing. He walks with you to the edge of the village.

But where should you look for Hiawatha? You remember the poem about Hiawatha, written by Henry Longfellow. Could he help?

Do you want to jump to 1855 to ask Longfellow for help? Turn to page 52.

Do you want to search in the forest? Turn to page 55.

The dream-guessing ceremony is sure to last a long time. You decide to play lacrosse.

You follow your new Turtle brother to a playing field. There is a set of goalposts at either end of the field. Several of the strongest Onondaga youths are already waiting.

"The object is to drive the ball through the Turtle goal," says Redwing, handing you a racquet. "You must not touch the ball. You carry it with the crosse stick, like this."

He scoops up the ball with the net at the end of his stick. Then he flings it into the air.

"Catch it, New Eyes," he yells.

You manage to catch the ball in your net, but it bounces out and falls to the ground.

"Not bad for your first time," says Redwing with a laugh.

"Pretty good for a Turtle," sneers a tall, husky Bear. "Let's play!"

The Turtles line up at the center of the field, facing the Bears. There are ten players on each side. You are at the end of the Turtle line. Redwing is in the middle, across from the husky Bear.

One of the elders drops the ball in the center and the game begins!

Redwing traps the ball! He flings it to a nearby Turtle and everyone begins to run.

Whooosh! The deerskin ball flies over your head and into the net of the young Bear brave. He takes off toward the Bears' goalposts.

Boom! The young Bear is down, tackled by another Turtle, and the ball is flying toward you! You catch it in your net!

"Here, New Eyes, throw it here!" It is Redwing. He is in the open near the Turtle goal.

You pitch the ball out of your net just as a huge Bear brings you to the ground.

Already running, Redwing snares the ball and springs for the Turtle goalposts. He scores!

A loud cheer goes up from the sidelines. It is Turtles 1, Bears 0.

You are out of breath and ready for a rest. Lacrosse is a rough game, but it is fun! Once again, the players line up at the center of the field.

Do you want to play more? Turn to page 61.

Do you want to go to the dream-guessing ceremony? Turn to page 46.

It is March 21, 1855. You are in a cozy study in Cambridge, Massachusetts. A man of about fifty is seated at a paper-strewn desk.

Peeking over the arm of a chair, you watch the man as he writes. He has thick muttonchop whiskers, and he wears a velvet-trimmed frock coat over a stiff shirt with a high white collar.

Suddenly he throws down his pen and jumps to his feet.

"It is done!" he cries happily. *"The Song of Hiawatha* is finished at last!" Grabbing a handful of pages, he hurries from the room.

"Fanny! Fanny, dear, listen to this!" he calls. You hear his footsteps going down a staircase as his voice fades.

Hurrying to the desk, you leaf through the huge pile of papers. What a long poem!

"By the shores of Gitche Gumee," you read,
"By the shining Big-Sea-Water,
Stood the wigwam of Nokomis,
Daughter of the Moon, Nokomis."

Wigwam? The Iroquois didn't live in wigwams. You skip a few pages.

"Homeward now went Hiawatha;
Pleasant was the landscape round him, . . .
In the land of the Dakotahs,
Where the Falls of Minnehaha . . ."

The land of the Dakotahs? Maybe you'd better start at the beginning.

"*The Song of Hiawatha,* by Henry Wadsworth Longfellow," you read. "Introduction."

"Should you ask me, whence these stories?
Whence these legends and traditions, . . .
I should answer, I should tell you,
From the forests and the prairies,
From the great lakes of the Northland,
From the land of the Ojibways, . . .
From the lips of Nawadaha, . . .
There he sang of Hiawatha . . ."

You stop reading. Longfellow's Hiawatha was a member of the Ojibway tribe. You're way off track.

And someone is coming. Hurry, you must jump in time.

Jump back to 1550. Go on to page 55.

You are walking along a well-worn trail deep in a forest. There are buds on the trees, and spring is in the air. But all at once the birds fall silent, and you hear mens' voices coming your way.

You leave the trail and hide behind a thick pine. The voices draw closer. You peek through the branches. It's a war party!

You hold your breath as a dozen fierce-looking warriors pass by. They are armed with arrows and war clubs, and their faces are striped with war paint. Once they are out of sight, you hurry on your way.

The trail curves, and you can hear running water up ahead. Soon you reach a wide stream. A short distance away, you can see smoke rising from the trees. You creep closer.

A single Iroquois has pulled his canoe out of the stream and has built a fire in a little clearing. He is kneeling at the fire, roasting a bird. Next to him are a bow and arrows. But he does not look like a warrior. He looks very kind, and he is singing a song of peace.

"Good day, young one," he says as you approach. He has not looked up from his task. "Won't you join me?"

"Thank you," you say, warming your hands at the fire. The stranger finishes roasting the bird. Then his eyes meet yours.

"I am called Deganawida," he says. "Peacemaker."

"They call me New Eyes," you reply.

Deganawida smiles. "An Iroquois name," he says. You nod proudly.

"Will you share my meal?" he asks.

You eat in friendly silence. Then Deganawida smiles again.

"Will you take some tobacco?" he offers, opening a pouch at his belt.

Do you take some tobacco? Turn to page 59.

Do you tell him you don't smoke? Turn to page 45.

It's the summer of 1780. You are in a smoking, ruined village. An old Iroquois woman is picking through the charred remains.

"What has happened?" you ask.

"Have you been left behind?" She sighs. "This was the home of Oneidas and Tuscaroras. We sided with the Colonists in their war with the British.

"Yesterday, Joseph Brant, the Mohawk colonel, came with his warriors to convince us to change sides. They burned the village. Many of our people have joined the British. But some have left for the American fort. This War of Independence has shattered the League. We have been caught in the middle of the whiteman's war. You can't stay here. You'll have to choose sides."

You certainly don't want to stay here. Your mission is to witness the founding of the Iroquois League, not the end of it!

You decide to jump back to 1550.

Jump back 230 years. Turn to page 55.

You nod politely. Deganawida gives you a pinch of tobacco. Then he takes a pinch himself and throws it onto the fire.

"For the spirits of the forest," he says.

"For the spirits of the forest," you repeat, casting the crumbled leaves into the flames. You watch as the blue smoke curls to the sky.

"Are you traveling alone?" you ask Deganawida. "It is dangerous. I have seen a war party not far from here."

"They are Atotarho's men," Deganawida answers gravely. "All of the villages in Iroquoia live in terror of the Onondaga wizard."

"They say he has snakes for hair!" you add.

Deganawida nods. "I have a vision of a Great Peace," he says. "But there is a man I must find. His name is Hiawatha."

You catch your breath. At last, someone who can help you!

"They say Hiawatha is a cannibal," Deganawida goes on. "They say he feasts on human flesh."

This doesn't sound like the Hiawatha you are looking for. The founder of the League of Five Nations couldn't have been a cannibal!

Should you continue your search with Deganawida? Or look elsewhere for a clue? Maybe the poet Longfellow could tell you if Hiawatha was a cannibal.

Do you want to consult Longfellow? Jump ahead to 1855. **Turn to page 52.**

Do you want to join Deganawida? **Turn to page 62.**

You are glad you decided to keep playing. Your muscles are sore, and your knees are black and blue, but the score is tied at four goals apiece. The next goal will win the contest.

The husky Bear has the ball, and he rushes at you like a charging bull.

"Block him!" shouts Redwing. You throw yourself into the path of the charging Bear, but another Bear grabs your ankles and brings you to the ground. Your crosse stick flies from your hand. The running Bear trips over your stick!

Redwing runs in to scoop up the ball in his net. He flings it away as the fallen Bear grabs at his knees. The Turtles score!

Redwing helps you up. You are both panting and muddy, but you can't stop laughing.

"Hooray for the Turtles!" you yell.

"Now for something more restful," Redwing says. "Let's go on to the dream-guessing!"

Turn to page 46.

"I'd like to go with you, if I may," you tell the Peacemaker.

"I would be pleased to have your company," Deganawida answers.

You walk for hours, listening as Deganawida sings his song of peace. It is a long, low chant with many verses.

Deganawida pauses to sniff the air. He motions you to walk softly.

Ahead of you is a small hut built of branches and mud. A thin finger of smoke curls upward through a hole in its roof. You can smell roasting meat.

A man comes to the narrow opening that serves as a door. He is a handsome brave with long black hair. He is gnawing at a piece of meat on a stick.

"Who disturbs Hiawatha's peace?" he asks gruffly.

"I am Deganawida," says your companion. "It is peace I hope to bring."

"And I am New Eyes," you say.

Hiawatha stares at you and turns to go back into his hut. Then he looks at you again, puzzled. "You remind me of someone I once met as a boy," he says. His eyes rest on the wooden

turtle you wear around your neck. "But maybe it was a dream."

Hiawatha nods to Deganawida. "You must have come far to find me," he says. The gruffness is gone from his voice. He beckons to you. "And I would not turn away my Turtle kin."

You enter the hut, staying close to the door. What if Hiawatha really is a cannibal? You are relieved to see that only a rabbit is roasting on the fire. Hiawatha grins.

"You have heard the cannibal story, I see," he says. "It helps to keep visitors away. I am but a peaceful hermit. Now, what is your purpose?"

Deganawida sits at the fire. "I have had a dream of a Great Pine Tree," he begins. "A Tree of Peace." The firelight flickers on his face as his voice grows strong.

"The Tree grows at the center of the world, at Onondaga. It reaches up to the Maker of Life, and its roots reach to the corners of the earth. They reach to the Mohawks and the Oneidas, to the Cayugas and the Senecas. The Five Nations must take shelter under the Great Tree. We must bury our weapons beneath its roots. We must become one great family.

"The Five Nations are like a longhouse, with five fires burning under one roof. We must spread the word of peace. This is my message."

"Your message is good," says Hiawatha. "I will help you spread the word of peace.

"And I will do more. I will find the wizard Atotarho. The Onondagas fear his power, and they obey his calls to war. We will never have peace until Atotarho agrees to join us under the Great Tree."

"Atotarho's mind is as tangled as the snakes he wears on his head," agrees Deganawida.

"*I* will straighten the mind of Atotarho," says Hiawatha. "I will go to Atotarho's village, and comb the snakes from the wizard's hair!"

"And I will spread the word of peace to the Five Nations," says Deganawida, "and invite them to meet at Lake Onondaga, beneath the Great Tree. We will meet at midsummer, when the air is sweet."

"And you, New Eyes?" says Hiawatha. "Will you come with your Turtle brother to the village of Atotarho? Or will you stay with the Peacemaker and help to spread his message?"

Do you want to stay with Deganawida? Turn to page 66.

Do you want to go with Hiawatha? Turn to page 73.

You decide to help Deganawida. You visit the villages of the Senecas and the Cayugas, the Mohawks and the Oneidas. They all agree to come to the meeting.

Finally, you return to the Onondaga village. It is very quiet. In the center of the village, you see a wooden post. It is painted bright red. And a bloodred tomahawk has been driven into its side.

"New Eyes! You're back!" Rainbow cries out.

"Where is everyone?" you ask.

"The braves have all gone on the warpath," Rainbow answers, pointing to the war post. "Atotarho has called the Onondagas to war."

"Have they not heard the words of peace?" you ask.

"We too want peace," Rainbow tells you. "But Atotarho wants war."

"That means Hiawatha has not yet reached the wizard," Deganawida says. "I will go to Atotarho. New Eyes, will you find Hiawatha and bring him to Atotarho's village?"

"I will," you answer.

**Help Hiawatha to face Atotarho.
Turn to page 73.**

You enter the village of the Onondaga wizard, Atotarho. People scurry to and fro, their voices hushed, their faces pale.

You can tell it is Atotarho. Inside a bark lodge in the center of the village, a man is yelling.

"I will see no one!" he shouts. "Begone, Peacemaker!" Atotarho's wicked laughter fills the village as a figure comes out the door of the lodge.

It's Deganawida! But the Peacemaker looks sad. His heart is heavy.

"Have you brought Hiawatha?" he asks.

"He has stopped at a stream in the forest," you reply. "I am to tell Atotarho that Hiawatha will come."

"I have told him so," says Deganawida. "He is furious. The snakes lash out from his head so that no one can get near him."

"What can we do?" you ask.

"We must gather every brave together," Deganawida answers. "We must teach them the song of peace. And then we must sing it. The song of peace will calm Atotarho's heart. Then

Hiawatha can get close enough to comb his hair and straighten his mind."

Men and women gather to hear Deganawida's words. Already, travelers have come from across the Five Nations.

Deganawida teaches everyone the song of peace. You have heard it so many times before, you think you could sing it backward. Then Deganawida calls for the bravest singers to come forward.

"You must sing perfectly, or the song will not work," he says. "And you must not hesitate. Pay no attention to the wizard's tricks."

"I will go first," says a Seneca brave. Singing the song of peace, he enters the lodge of Atotarho. But as he disappears, a bolt of lightning flashes through the door! The Seneca brave runs out after it.

"I will go next," says a Cayuga woman. But as she passes through the door, a shower of hailstones chases her back.

An Oneida tries next. But his singing is drowned in a roar of thunder, and he too fails.

"Let me try," you say to Deganawida.

"All right, New Eyes," he says. "Remember, the wizard creates only illusions."

Slowly you enter the lodge. You sing at the top of your lungs, and you keep your eyes shut.

Thunder and lightning flash around you, but you sing and sing, not daring to peek.

The inside of the lodge sounds like the Fourth of July, but you continue to sing. Then Deganawida's voice joins yours.

Inside the lodge, it grows quiet. You keep on singing and open your eyes.

The wizard Atotarho is seated against the far wall of the lodge, and he is a terrible sight! He is huge and powerful and is clad only in a loincloth. Snakes writhe from his headdress like living hair. A great war club rests in his lap.

Atotarho fixes you with an evil stare, but he cannot move! Still you sing the song of peace.

You feel a movement behind you. *Hiawatha!*

Deganawida draws closer to the wizard. Atotarho is as still as a statue. The song is working!

You continue to sing as Hiawatha moves forward. He is holding a basket and a comb carved of shell. He touches the comb to Atotarho's headdress. It catches on a snake, and he tosses the twisting reptile into the basket. Then he combs out another one. And another. Deganawida stops singing. You stop, too.

"Atotarho, great leader of the Onondagas," says Deganawida. "I bring a message of peace."

"I have heard your message, Peacemaker," Atotarho answers. "And it is good. My mind

has been twisted and wrong. But He Who Combs has straightened my thoughts. The Onondagas will host the meeting of the Five Nations. We will bury our weapons beneath the Great Tree."

There is to be peace at last!

"You have been brave beyond words, New Eyes," says Hiawatha.

"Please join us at the Council of the Five Nations," says Deganawida. "The people will come from across the land, to meet at midsummer beneath the Great Tree."

"I will be honored," you tell your Iroquois brothers. You are very proud.

Jump ahead to midsummer, 1550.
Turn to page 77.

Hiawatha is walking in the woods near his hut. He seems uneasy.

"Why do we not go to face Atotarho now?" you ask. "Are you afraid?"

"I am not afraid, New Eyes," answers the brave. "But there is something I must do first."

"What is it?" you ask.

"I do not know. But come, we will begin our journey. I will listen to the forest until it tells me what I must do."

You walk in silence for a while. But soon your curiosity loosens your tongue.

"Why did you become a hermit?" you ask.

"The Onondagas live in fear of Atotarho," answers Hiawatha. "My heart was heavy with so much killing. So I moved to the forest. But now we have a chance to walk the path of peace."

"We must face this evil wizard right away," you say. "Listen. I hear a stream."

"It is the stream that leads to Atotarho's village," says Hiawatha. "Come."

Hiawatha kneels by the stream. He reaches into the water and pulls out a handful of mud.

Then he rinses whatever he is holding. It's a shell!

"Look!" says Hiawatha excitedly. "It is white on one side and purple on the other. Help me to find more!"

You squat next to the Iroquois brave and dig for shells in the muddy stream. Soon you have a pile of glistening shells.

Hiawatha begins to break the shells into small pieces with a sharp rock. Then he rubs them between his hands with grains of sand. Soon the pieces of shell are smoothed and rounded, like beads.

Next, he uses a pointed stick and a piece of flint to drill a hole through each piece of shell. It takes a very long time.

"What are you doing?" you ask. "Shouldn't we face Atotarho now?"

"Find me some slender rushes," says Hiawatha. "Over there." He points to a patch of weeds growing at the edge of the stream. He does not answer your question.

You fetch a handful of the weeds. Hiawatha strings the shells on the stems of the rushes, like strings of beads.

"*Wampumpeag*," murmurs Hiawatha. He looks up at you. "*Umpeag* means things that are strung," he explains. "*Wamp* means white. *Wampum*."

Your face breaks into a grin. Wampum!

"Here, New Eyes," says Hiawatha. He hands you an extra bead. "Put this in your pouch."

You pocket the smooth white bead.

"But what will you use them for?" you ask.

"I will speak the thoughts of my people into the strings of wampum," answers the brave. "And the wampum will help us to remember our words and speak them back. Wampum will hold words of truth, and these words we will never forget."

You finger the little bead in your pouch. Your mission is almost complete! But Hiawatha must still face the Onondaga wizard.

Hiawatha stands and stretches.

"I am ready to face Atotarho," he says. "You must go to his village and tell him I am coming. Then I will comb the snakes from his hair and untwist his twisted mind."

"I will go," you tell Hiawatha.

"Thank you, brave New Eyes," says Hiawatha. He sits calmly by the stream and begins to look for more shells.

Are you ready to face Atotarho? Turn to page 68.

It is the middle of the summer of 1550. You are sitting in the shade of a huge tree on the shore of Lake Onondaga. Rainbow sits on one side of you, and Redwing sits on the other.

The lakeside is crowded with Iroquois from all five tribes, arranged in a circle around the Great Tree. Deganawida rises to speak.

"I welcome you, my sisters and brothers, to the Council Fire of the Five Nations, at the tree of great peace," says the Peacemaker.

"In each nation," he continues, "there are men of wisdom. These men will be chosen to be the chiefs of their people by the clan mothers, the wisest women of each tribe. We shall live as one family beneath the roof of a great long-house. The Onondagas are to be the Keepers of the Central Fire. The Mohawks will be the Keepers of the Eastern Door, and the Senecas will be the Keepers of the Western Door.

"Now let us bury our hatchets beneath the Tree of Peace. We will fight among ourselves no more."

A joyous cheer goes up from the crowd as the leaders of the Five Nations cast their war clubs into a hole beneath the roots of the Great Tree.

The League of Five Nations has been born!

The crowd falls silent once more. Hiawatha has risen to speak.

"I have a gift for the People of the Longhouse," he says. He unrolls a long, wide belt. It has a white design on a purple ground. And it is woven completely of shells!

"Into this wampum I have spoken the truth of the Great Peace." Hiawatha points to the designs on the belt.

"At the center is the heart. It is also the Great Tree. The Great Peace is lodged in the heart of the Five Nations, here at Onondaga.

"The white squares nearest the heart stand for the Oneidas and the Cayugas. The outermost squares are the Keepers of the Doorways, the Mohawks and the Senecas.

"The lines connecting the Five Nations go to the ends of the earth. Any nation wishing to follow the Path of Peace may join with the People of the Longhouse and take shelter under our roof.

"The color white stands for peace, equality, and love. May these qualities govern our hearts as we sit at the Council Fire."

The People of the Longhouse rise together. "*Na-ho,*" they say in one voice. "May it be so."

Hiawatha nods at you and smiles.

"I wish to thank my brave and patient friend,

New Eyes, who helped me to find the wampum shells you see in this belt. Maybe we should rename him Shell Finder."

"Na-ho!" shout the people.

Then Atotarho comes your way. *"Na-ho,* New Eyes," he says with a grin. "I too must thank you, for your powerful singing voice! Maybe we should rename you Fearless Singer!"

Deganawida joins in.

"I thank you most of all," says the Peacemaker, "for your feet have walked the Path of Peace. Perhaps we should rename you Little Peacemaker!"

Everyone laughs, and you join in the celebration.

Mission Completed.

About the Contributors

CAROL GASKIN has written six previous books for young readers, including the Forgotten Forest series: *The War of the Wizards, The Magician's Ring, The Forbidden Towers,* and *The Master of Mazes.* She is also the author of Time Machine # 13, *Secret of the Royal Treasure.* She recently moved from a small apartment in New York City to a house in Sarasota, Florida, where she has sighted an alligator in her yard at least once.

JOSÉ ORTIZ is a Spanish artist best known for his fantasy and science-fiction illustrations. He began his career as a popular magazine artist at the age of nineteen, creating such notable characters as Sigur the Viking. In the 1970s his work gained recognition in the U.S. He was awarded the Warren Prize for illustration in 1975. He is currently preparing a new series, *Hombre,* for *Cimoc* magazine.